Charles William Sommerville

Robert Goodloe Harper

Charles William Sommerville

Robert Goodloe Harper

ISBN/EAN: 9783744660457

Printed in Europe, USA, Canada, Australia, Japan

Cover: Foto ©Raphael Reischuk / pixelio.de

More available books at **www.hansebooks.com**

Robert Goodloe Harper

BY

C. W. SOMMERVILLE, A. M.

A Dissertation presented to the Board of University Studies
of the Johns Hopkins University for the
Degree of Doctor of Philosophy.

———

THE NEALE COMPANY
481 ELEVENTH STREET N. W.
WASHINGTON, D. C.
1899

TO MY SISTERS.

Of those distinguished men who graced the Maryland bar in the early part of this century, General Robert Goodloe Harper ranked among the first. It is the aim of this paper to set forth the main facts in his life in its public and national relations. Materials for this purpose were abundant, but scattered. They included a brief manuscript account of his life written by General Harper about 1801; files of letters and documents, to which access was given by Mr. W. C. Pennington, of Baltimore; two volumes of Harper's Works (Baltimore, 1814), and sundry pamphlets published by him. Further information was gathered from newspapers, journals, biographies and reports.

My thanks for suggestions are due to Professor Adams, to Drs. Steiner, Vincent, Ballagh and Willoughby.

Baltimore, June, 1899.

ROBERT GOODLOE HARPER,

By C. W. Sommerville.

ROBERT GOODLOE HARPER was born on a Virginia farm near Fredericksburg, in January, 1765. His father, Jesse Harper, and his grandfather, Abraham Harper, had lived for years in Spottsylvania County, Va. The family is traced far back in English history. In Virginia its members had intermarried with the Minors and the Goodloes.

Robert Goodloe Harper was the only boy in a family of nine. When he was about four years old his father moved into Northern North Carolina, and there the family has remained. Harper was taught at home until about his tenth year, when he was sent to the grammar school.

When the Bristish Army, under Lord Cornwallis, having defeated General Gates near Camden, overran North Carolina, Harper, though but a lad of fifteen, left his books and joined a volunteer corps of cavalry, which served under General Nathaniel Greene, until the British left the State for Yorktown.

Harper now tried to study again, but he found books too dull after an experience in the field of arms, and after the promotion his efforts had gained. He had been made Quartermaster to his corps.* His efforts at study were made the harder by a tempting offer of a lieutenancy in a regular cavalry regiment. His father dissuaded him from accepting the lieutenancy, and Harper agreed to continue his studies until he was twenty years old, on his father's promise then to equip him for military service.

Peace with England soon relieved the father of his part of the agreement, and a surveying tour in 1783 in "the Kentucky and Tennessee countries" took Harper away from books again. This visit to the West gave Harper a knowledge of that great territory and also a turn for land specula-

---

*R. Walsh, Jr., in "Encyclopedia Americana." Walsh had read law in Harper's office.

The facts in this chapter are found in unpublished manuscripts, to which I have had access through the courtesy of Mr. W. C. Pennington, of Baltimore.

tion; facts which influenced his future to some degree. He acquired at this time some of the western lands, but from surveyors' frauds and his own neglect little profit came of them.

For some time after his return from the West, Harper indulged in idleness, dissipation and gambling. Finally he accepted his father's offer to send him to college, and in June, 1784, he set out for Princeton College, N. J. When his slender means were exhausted, he applied to President John Witherspoon for employment in a grammar school which the President had established in the college. Rev. Dr. Samuel Stanhope Smith also engaged him to teach some boys who had been put in Dr. Smith's care. This work in teaching consumed eight hours a day, so that when college duties were done there was little time left for rest or exercise. In the spring vacation of 1785 Harper went to New York and had an interview with Governor Spaight, of North Carolina, who loaned the student means for the next session at college. Harper carried the junior and senior classes together the next term, and on September 28, 1785, he was graduated Bachelor of Arts, received the Essayist's Medal, and delivered a discourse on "The Proper Objects of Education."*

When Harper left college it was his desire to see the world. He went with a fellow student to Philadelphia and determined to sail for England and make the tour of Europe on foot. He planned to give lessons in London and to use his knowledge of tools, if need be, at the joiner's trade, until his means were better. But ice in the Delaware delayed shipping for weeks.†

This delay was fatal to Harper's plan, and he determined to go to Charleston, S. C., and teach and study law.

As Harper stood a penniless stranger on the Charleston wharf in November, 1785, he was accosted by the father of one of his former pupils at Princeton, and received great kindness and help from him. In Charleston he engaged as usher in a large school kept by Mr. Thompson. He thus made forty guineas a year and at the same time studied law in the office of two young Parkers, who were then making a reputation at the bar. Colonel Hawkins, of North Carolina, was in Charleston during the winter, and having known the Harpers, introduced Robert Goodloe Harper to General

*New Jersey Gazette, October 10, 1780, quoted by Moore in his "American Eloquence," page 489.
†Robert Walsh, Jr., in "Encyclopedia Americana."

Pinckney, Mr. Edward Rutledge and other persons of prominence. In the fall of 1786, Harper was admitted to the bar. He soon located in Ninety-six District, in the upper part of South Carolina. Here he gained some political notice by a series of articles on a proposed change in the State Constitution.*

In the latter part of 1789, Harper removed to Charleston, where he engaged in a growing practice, and was soon in the State Legislature.

In 1791 he renewed his connection with land speculation, then rife. A company which had contracted with the State of Georgia† for a large territory on the Mississippi engaged him as their manager, offering him five per cent. of the purchase for his services. He went that summer to Philadelphia to sell the stock of this land company.

The land scheme miscarried, but Harper's mind had been diverted from his profession, and his trip had created a decided relish for the Northern States, and had aroused ambitions towards a Congressional career.

A seat was offered Harper in 1792, but he declined because of the small pay of six dollars per diem allowed Representatives. Meanwhile land speculation was profitable and very attractive.

In 1794 he bought a plantation in Ninety-six, intending to remove there from Charleston. He then offered himself a candidate for the House of Representatives and was elected for Ninety-six District, meanwhile continuing in the Legislature of the State until the time for him to take his seat in Congress, December, 1795. Before this time arrived the death of Alexander Gillon caused a vacancy in the Orangeburg District. Harper was pressed to stand as a candidate for Orangeburg. He was elected as a Democrat, and took his seat on Monday, February 9, 1795.‡

In the importance of events and discussions, excitements of parties and the talents of leaders, that period may be termed one of the most remarkable in our annals as a nation. Harper was to take his place among the leaders of the dominant party. Madison wrote to Jefferson on learning of Harper's first election (November 16, 1794): "Hunter's successor (a Mr. Harper) will be a valuable acquisition, being able, sound and eloquent."§

*Harper's Works, 1: 42.
†Out of this grew the famous Yazoo frauds so long fought by John Randolph, of Roanoke.
‡Annals of Congress, 1793-'5, page 1205.
§Madison's Works 2: 20.

On Monday, February 9, 1790, Harper took his seat in Congress as a Representative of South Carolina,* and on the 17th he was assigned to his first committee.† We shall find him advocating measures of relief, internal improvements and of general welfare. His view extended to the whole country. In 1791 a survey of the coast of Georgia had been begun by private persons. Harper saw the utility of such a survey to shipping, and at once advocated a loan by the United States for completing such a work, because it was for the national benefit.‡ He rose above narrow state lines before harbor improvements or coast survey by the National Government had been thought of.

His experience with land speculations enabled him to give a complete historical argument vindicating the right of Georgia in the famous Yazoo land frauds,§ and in case of the Northwest Territory he opposed the sale of lands in large tracts to speculators. He was unsuccessful in his opposition, but he was on the side of wisdom, for he advocated the sale of lands in small lots to actual settlers. This would shut out speculators, give the Government a better price for them, and insure permanent and desirable settlers.‖

Harper's entrance into Congress was in the midst of the negotiations with England regarding the differences left unsettled since the treaty of Paris, 1783. Jay's treaty was signed November 19, 1794, but it did not reach Washington until March 7, 1795. When its provisions were known opposition to it swept the country with the violence of a hurricane.¶ Jefferson called it infamous; Jay was burned in effigy. As an appropriation was necessary to carry the treaty into effect, it had to come before the House. This brought out notable speeches.** Washington refused to send the papers asked for, because the treaty-making power, he said, laid with the Executive with the Senate's consent. Torrents of abuse fell on Washington. There was talk of impeachment. Speeches were fiery. "Never," said Marshall, "had a greater display been made of argument, of eloquence and of passion." One of the greatest speeches was by Fisher Ames. Gallatin asserted†† that a treaty is not valid until it

*Annals 1793-5, 1205.
†Annals, 1230.
‡Annals, 1793-5; p. 1249, and for 1795-6, pp. 149-158.
§Annals, 1795-6, p. 1279.
‖Annals, 1795-6; p. 353.
¶Whitelock, Life and Times of John Jay, p. 278.
**Annals, 1795-6; pp. 457, 747, 801, 886, 810, 955, 1171.
††Annals, p. 747.

has received the sanction of the House. Harper replied that in limited governments the treaty-making power may be limited. The treaty-making power had been given to the President and Senate, as legislative power to the House. A treaty is not a law and does not belong to the House. A treaty derives its origin from the consent of equals, while a law gets its from the authority of a superior. Laws are commands; treaties are compacts.

Treaties, he argued, lie in the province of the law of nations; the legislative power has to do with municipal law. The Legislature cannot make a compact, nor can the treaty-making power make a law. The House had nothing to do with treaties except to determine how far they could carry them out. Harper supported his views by citations from English and international usage. With as forcible arguments he maintained against Gallatin that treaties repeal all existing opposing laws.*

In defense of Jay's treaty Harper argued that the whole commercial part of it was to expire at the end of twelve years and might be terminated by the United States at the end of two years from the close of the war between England and France. Hard as the stipulations might be, they could not ruin trade in so short a while. We charged England with having failed to give up the western posts, as she had agreed to do in the treaty of Paris; with having carried away, contrary to that treaty, a number of slaves, when New York was evacuated, and with violating the law of nations by the capture of American vessels which were neutral in regard to England and France. But England claimed to hold the posts as a pledge for our payment of British debts; that the negroes carried away were not American property at this time, and that no American vessel had been taken against the law of nations. Now, said Harper, under these circumstances, there were but three courses to follow: Submit quietly; compel redress; negotiate redress. The first course would be dastardly. The second course might take the direction of war, commercial restriction, prohibition of intercourse, or sequestration of debts. As to war, we had not a frigate nor a regiment to spare from the Indian wars, commercial restriction would probably widen the breach,† and we would lose more than we gained. To suspend commercial intercourse would hurt us and do no good; and, finally, se-

*Annals, 1795-6; p. 758.
†Works 1: 12.

questration of British debts would shake foreign confidence in us, ruin our credit and at the last compel us to fight or to negotiate under less favorable circumstances. The third course, negotiation, was then the only possible course left us. More than this, he said, things were not as bad as they appeared to be. The negroes carried off numbered only about three throusand, and a third of these were free. The two thousand slaves at two hundred dollars each would make a sum far less than the cost of a quarrel; a three months' war would cost five times as much. The impressment of seamen was really provided against in the nineteenth article of the treaty.* Then the Western posts were to be held only for eighteen months longer. These drawbacks could be endured for a while rather than to suffer all the horrors of war.

Moreover, the treaty settled our differences, gave us advantages in the East Indies and Canadian trade, and was a basis for a future and more beneficial arrangement.

In spite of many such arguments the appropriation bill necessary to render the treaty effective only passed by a vote of 51 to 48. All the New England members but four, most of those from the Middle States, but only four from the South, voted for the bill. Harper was serving his first term, and was placing his future political advancement in jeopardy by opposing the popular will, almost unanimous in the South, which had wrought itself up to the pitch of stoning Hamilton for attempting to defend the treaty.† But Harper was too brave to go against his convictions. He defended the treaty and published his arguments for it. His straightforward course insured his re-election until the downfall of the Federalists.

In the Fifth and Sixth Congresses, Harper was the Federalist leader.‡ He was made Chairman of the Committee on Ways and Means December 4, 1797,§ and was again appointed December 9, 1799, for the last session he served. In this position he had charge of all the financial schemes of the Administration at the critical period of the threatened war with France.

In 1797, Harper published his "Observations on the Dispute Between the United States and France," in which he presented a very strong case against France. The publica-

*Works 1: 18.
†MacMaster, United States, 2: 219.
‡Schouler, Hist. of the U. S., 1: 352.
§Annals of Congress, 1797, p. 672, and 1799, p. 197.

tion brought him much notice. Peter Porcupine,* in a tirade against Harper, says that "the pamphlet which gained him so much renown in England, and which was quoted with high encomiums in both Houses of Parliament, I furnished the hints, gave the materials, drew the plan for; and while Lord Grenville was extolling this pamphlet in one House and Mr. Dundas in the other, while they were paying such a handsome tribute to the talents, candor and integrity of the honorable member of the American Congress, after the English applause had been echoed and re-echoed through America, Harper published a new edition. The pamphlet did great good in both countries and great injury to France." G. Cabot wrote, April 25, 1798, to John Adams:† "We keep our presses going with Harper's excellent speech and pamphlet. Harper must devote himself to proving to the people the absolute propriety of what is done. If he knew the extent of his fame already acquired, his ambition would stimulate him to the most laborious undertakings;" also,‡ quoting a letter from William Smith, Minister to Portugal, August 14, 1798, "Harper's pamphlet has been translated into Portuguese and distributed here gratis. It was printed by order of the Government." Fisher Ames wrote to Chris. Gore in London, July 28, 1798:§ "Did Lord Grenville and Dundas know that their eulogium on his book would help the French by marring a good thing in Congress? Yet, so it is. Harper is a fine fellow, but praise has half spoiled him."

The impeachment of Blount occupied a part of this session of Congress, and Harper took a leading part in the case. An account of it is given below.

The protective measures of proposed restriction in naturalization, the Alien Act, Alien Enemies Act and the Sedition Act were all championed by Harper. In advocating the limitation of naturalization facilities, he said|| it was time we should recover from the mistake of admitting foreigners to citizenship. This mistake had been productive of very great evils to the country, and there was danger of those evils increasing. The time had come when it was proper to declare that nothing but birth should entitle a man to citizenship in this country. He was for giving foreigners every facility for acquiring and holding property and of transfer-

*Porcupine's Works, 9; 331.
†Life and Works of Fisher Ames, 1: 236.
‡2, 119.
§Ibid, 1: 236.
||Annals, 1798; p. 1567.

ring it to their families, but they should not be given the right of citizenship, because they could not have the same views as native citizens. It was an underlying principle of civil society that none but persons born in a country should be permitted to take part in the government. The bill favoring a more restricted naturalization became law June 18.[*]

One of Harper's last speeches in Congress[†] was in advocacy of continuing the Sedition Act, which he regarded "as a shield for the liberty of the press and the freedom of opinion. "I wish," he said, "to interpose this law between the freedom of discussion and the overbearing sway of that tyrannical spirit by which a certain political party[‡] in this country is actuated, which arrogates to itself to speak in the name of the people, knows neither moderation, mercy, nor justice, regards neither feeling, principle, nor right, and sweeps down with relentless fury all that dares detect its follies, oppose its progress or resist its domination." The Sedition Act, he thought, was the one barrier that stood between Democratic fury and public liberty. Harper's whole career had been marked by the same zealous support of Administration measures, of ample military and naval preparation as the surest means of protection and respect abroad, and of avoiding encroachments, especially by France.

Upon the close of his Congressional career (March 5, 1801), Harper set forth a review of his and his party's course in Congress. The change which occurred March 4, 1801, was the first in our history of one party's giving place to another. For twelve years the Federalists had been in power; with Jefferson the trial was to be made of something new. "Should Mr. Jefferson conduct the Government on rational principles," Harper wrote to a friend in South Carolina, "and with steadiness, vigor and prudence, his elevation will prove a public blessing. The fear that he might not was a sufficient reason for opposing his election." He had no love for the Democrats, and dwells upon the work of "The Federal Republicans or Federalists," by whom the affairs of the United States have been successfully managed, the friends and associates of Washington, the supporters of Adams, and the authors of the Federal Government itself, and of that system of domestic and foreign policy by which this nation has been conducted with unexampled rapidity in the course of honor, prosperity and happiness. These are the men whose system

---

[*]W. Macdonald, Select Documents of U. S. Hist., p. 138.
[†]Jan. 21, 1801, Annals, p. 940.
[‡]The Republicans.

I adopted from my first entrance into public life, with whom it was my pride and boast to have stood, and with whom I wish to fall, if fall they must.

The leading principle of this system as to foreign nations had been to preserve peace with all, but to grant privileges to none, and to submit to indignities from none, relying for the protection of our rights not on the good will of other governments, but on our own strength. "By these principles," said Harper, "we have maintained the nation in peace, through the most general and furious war of modern times. England and France were both endeavoring to draw us into it. We resisted both and surmounted all difficulties without an abandonment of national rights or honor. We have established a navy which has averted the war, and still protects our commerce. With Spain we have settled a territorial dispute on terms honorable and advantageous to our nation."

In domestic concerns Harper had supported the authority of the Federal Government, which alone, he thought, was capable of insuring our safety from abroad by opposing a united strength, and of maintaining peace at home by checking the ambition of the states. It was of prime importance to make the Federal Government as independent as possible of state influence. In every struggle between the Federal and the State Governments, Harper considered the State Governments as possessing the greater natural strength, and therefore thought it his duty to take the part of the weaker party. For the same reason he supported the Executive against the encroachment of the Legislature.

A maxim of Harper's was that public officials could not be induced to accept public trust unless they could be decently maintained by the office. Otherwise it would be difficult to prevail on men of the highest character to accept office. To compensate handsomely all the chief officers of Government would cost less than incompetent men might waste in a month.

For revenue commerce is necessary. Harper said nine millions derived from imposts cost less and were less than four hundred thousand gotten from a whisky tax. For encouraging trade he had advocated establishment of banks, encouragement of insurance companies, formation of commercial treaties, sending consuls to trading countries, erection of lighthouses, harbor improvements and coast defenses. These had been his principles. In the momentary eclipse of these principles by Republican success, when it was said the sun of Federalism had set forever, Harper did not lose hope.

With confidence he prophesied the final triumph of Federalism. "The sun of Federalism may set," he said, "but it will rise again. The mists of Democracy may obscure it for a moment, but they cannot tarnish its lustre, much less extinguish its light. It may set, but the benighted nation, after tossing for a while in the disturbed dream of fancied good, will wake to mourn its absence, and sigh for its return. It will return. The nation shall hail its approach and rejoice in the brightness of its course. Names may change, the men who hold the reins may be different, the denomination of parties may be altered or forgotten, but the principles on which the Federalists have acted must be adopted and their plans must be pursued or the Government must fall to pieces."

There have been seven trials on impeachment under the Constitution of the United States. In the first three of these cases Harper participated, once as one of the managers on the part of the House of Representatives and twice as counsel for the impeached. These early cases were particularly important, because they established precedents. Impeachment having been borrowed from the English Constitution, and having been more or less loosely defined in its nature and limits, there arose in the United States uncertainty as to how much change was necessary in the institution as it existed in England. There are two schools of interpretation. One holds that the power of impeachment extends only to such offenders as may afterwards be indicted according to law. This was Harper's view. The other view is that "high crimes and misdemeanors" embrace not only indictable offenses, but also those wider and vaguer political offenses not to be reached by the ordinary law.

The first impeachment to occur under the present Constitution was that of Senator Blount, of Tennessee.* Blount had been in the Continental Congress and had been Governor of the Southwest Territory. He aimed at the establishment of a colony back of the Alleghenies in English interests. Congress felt that unless Blount's schemes were stamped with infamy the country would fall to pieces.†

Blount had great favor with the Indians and the people of Tennessee, who looked to the Mississippi for an outlet for

---

*Wharton, State Trials, p. 317; Annals of Congress, 1797-8.

†Wm. Cobbett's "Peter Porcupine," and Schouler History of the United States, 1: 304.

their trade. He was therefore important if disaffected towards the United States. The treaty with Spain in 1795 was considered very advantageous to the Western Territory. But it was feared that a secret article in a treaty between Spain and France had ceded Louisiana to France. Blount did not like the idea of having the French for neighbors, because they would interfere with the settlement of Western lands and some of his own lands. He therefore planned to put the English in possession of Louisiana and the Floridas, if England would hold New Orleans, while he, at the head of settlers and Indians, drove the Spaniards from North America and prevented the French settling in Louisiana. A letter of Blount's, which implicated him in these treasonable schemes* was put into the President's hands, and was read in the Senate in Blount's presence. He was arrested and impeached (July 7, 1797). Harper was made one of the committee to prepare the articles of impeachment. Blount was twice bailed to answer the charges, but on July 8, 1797, he was expelled from the Senate, having been guilty of a high misdemeanor.† The managers, however, proceeded with the collection of evidence. January 9, 1798, the articles were agreed to. They charged Blount with setting on foot a military expedition against Spain in the interest of England, inciting the Indians against the Spaniards in the Floridas and injuring the United States among the Indians. The trial did not occur until December 17, 1798. Blount did not appear. Harper wished to follow the precedent of the English law requiring the presence of the accused.‡ He wished the Senate to compel Blount's presence. He was not supported in this.§ On December 24 Ingersoll and Dallas appeared for Blount and urged a lack of jurisdiction, as impeachment is permitted only against the President or any civil officer of the United States, and that a Senator is not a civil officer. An officer may not avoid punishment by resigning his office.|| But Blount had been expelled. There was, therefore, no jurisdiction. The reply of the managers was that a Senator is a civil officer, and that impeachment is a purely political proceeding, aiming not so much at the punishment of the offender as the security of the State. Harper's argument is chiefly upon the point whether a Sena-

*Porcupine's Works, 9: 143.
†Wharton, State Trials, p. 200.
‡Foster on the Constitution, 1: 1.
§Annals of Congress, December 21, 1798.
||This was the point involved in the Belknap case.

tor is a civil officer.* It was contended by Bayard and Harper that the nature, object and extent of impeachment must be sought in the common law of England, whence it was derived. Dallas exclaimed: "Shall we, in order to decide questions respecting our dearest rights, have recourse to the dark and barbarous volumes of the common law?"† This epithet applied to the common law was caught up by Harper and used to great effect. "This," he said, addressing Vice-President Jefferson, who presided over the impeachment court, "reminds me of the worm-eaten volumes of the law of nations of which we heard so much in our dispute with the French Republic. Citizen Genet, when he found himself hard pressed by the authorities from the law of nations which our Secretary of State (Jefferson) adduced against him, denied the authority of Grotius, Puffendorf and Vattel and called their works 'worm-eaten volumes,' whose contents, he thanked God, he had long since forgotten. So the ingenious counsel for the defense, unable to answer or evade the arguments from the common law, gets rid of them at once by a coup-de-main a la Genet, and consigns them to oblivion as dark and barbarous volumes unworthy of the light of the new philosophy." Harper proceeds at length to show how the common law of England underlies the whole of our jurisprudence, and affects the most vital issues of our life, always ringing the changes on the "dark and barbarous volumes of the common law." He supported the jurisdiction of the Senate in this case, and replied to the objection that no person but an officer of the United States is liable to impeachment, and that a Senator is not a civil officer. When a term as impeachment, he contended, is taken without explanation into our Constitution, every question respecting its meaning must be decided by a reference to the code from whence it was drawn. All that our Constitution provides for is, by whom impeachments shall be preferred; by whom and in what manner the impeached shall be tried, and what shall be the punishment. In no case shall punishment go beyond removal from office and disqualification; and in the case of the President and the Vice-President and all civil officers it shall not stop short of removal. But as to the persons who shall be impeached, besides those just mentioned, or as to the offenses for which they may be impeached, not a word is to be found in the Con-

---

*Wharton, State Trials, 1: 296, et sq.
†Dallas had been educated in England at the Temple.

stitution. The term was intended to have the same mean‧
ing, extent and force as it has in the common law of Eng‧
land. In that law the power of impeachment is unlimited,
and extends to every person and every officer.* Blount was
then impeachable. But granting that impeachment is lim‧
ited to officers of the Government, a Senator is an officer,
and so is liable to impeachment. It is not true that none
but civil officers are liable to impeachment. The Constitu‧
tion contradicts that. In the case of the President and
Vice-President or any civil officer, it was provided that pun‧
ishment should not be less than removal, though it might
be more. The distinction between civil officers and other
officers may have arisen from an opinion that there might
be danger under some circumstances in removing from his
command a military officer whom it might, however, be
proper to censure or suspend. As to military officers, there‧
fore, a complete discretion was left to the Senate, but not as
to civil officers. They, on conviction, must be removed.
Military officers may or may not be removed, according to
circumstances. Had the Constitution intended otherwise it
would have provided that all civil officers and no other per‧
sons shall be liable to impeachment. But if it can be shown
that a Senator is an officer of the United States and that a
seat in the Senate is an office, it will follow that the defend‧
ant is liable to impeachment. Harper then goes on to prove
that a Senator is an officer and a civil officer of the United
States. The Constitution, he held, uses the term office in
the most general sense. According to its derivation office
signified duty or employment. If the duties relate to the
Civil Government, the office is a civil office. A Senator is a
civil officer, since he holds a post which requires the per‧
formance of some duty of a public nature relating to the
Civil Government. As the duties of the President comprise
both the civil and the military departments, he would not
have been included in the designation civil officer. It was,
therefore, necessary to name him expressly. It is only nec‧
essary to show that a Senator is an officer of the United
States. The contention that a Senator cannot be considered
an officer because there could be no quo warranto to remove
him from his place nor mandamus to place him in it is of no
force, since the same thing applies to the President, Judges,
Secretaries and Commander-in-Chief of the Army. A Sena‧
tor, then, was, in Harper's view, a civil officer of the United

*Dr. Sacheverell was impeached in 1709 for preaching a certain
sermon. Foster on the Constitution, p. 1: 590; Lecky, Hist. Eng., 1:
51 sq.

States and so liable to impeachment. Senator Blount
should therefore be tried under the articles preferred against
him.*   When the vote was taken (January 10) it was decided
(14 to 11) that Blount was not impeachable, because he was
not a civil officer of the United States. January 25, 1798,
Mr. Jefferson wrote to Mr. Madison that "Blount's affair is
to come on next. This will be made the occasion of offering
a clause for the introduction of juries into these trials."
(February 8). "But many great preliminary questions will
arise. Must not a formal law settle the oath of the Senator?
Form of pleadings, process against persons and goods. May
he not appear by attorney? Must he not be tried by jury?
Is a Senator impeachable? Is an ex-Senator impeachable?†
Harper's position in this first impeachment case was: 1, the
impeached must be present; 2, his presence may be compelled; 3, a Senator is a civil officer of the United States and
is liable to impeachment; 4, the impeached cannot escape
trial by resignation or expulsion. On the first and second
points the Senate decided against Harper; on the third, also,
but the decision has not been wholly acquiesced in. The
fourth point was not passed upon, but Harper's position was
sound, and was the view held by the majority of the court
in the Belknap case.

The second impeachment in the history of the United
States was that of Judge John Pickering, of the Federal
District Court of New Hampshire. This case has appealed
to the sympathies of many. It appealed to Harper, who had
now retired from Congress, and was gaining eminence at the
bar. The articles of impeachment presented by Nicholson
and John Randolph, of Roanoke,‡ charged irregular proceedings in Admiralty Jurisdiction and loose morals and
intemperate habits.§

*It appears that all that Harper proved was that members of the
State Legislatures were officers of the State choosing them. He did
not prove that the Senator from a State is an officer of the United
States Government. Blount contended that a Senator is an officer
of the State choosing him, but not of the United States, by whom
he was not chosen. Harper's attempt to explain Art. 1, Sec. 6, of
the Constitution was also futile.

†February 15. Cf. Ford's Edition of the writings of Jefferson, 7:
192 to 193; 198 to 199: 202 to 203.

‡March 3, 1803, Annals of Congress, 1803-4, p. 15.

§The testimony in the case is very graphic; see Annals of Congress, 1803-4, p. 351. Judge Pickering had declared in the Admiralty
case "that he could finish the business in four minutes." I am ——
drunk, but I will be sober by morning." The attorney said he claimed
an appeal The judge replied, "Appeal and be ——." He gave the

March 2, 1804, Judge Pickering was called three times, but he did not appear.* Instead, a letter was presented from Harper, enclosing a petition from Pickering and begging that the trial be deferred. Harper appeared at the request of Judge Pickering's son to support the petition, if he should be allowed to do so. The son was too poor to send witnesses, and Judge Pickering's insanity prevented his taking any action. For these reasons Harper begged the privilege of acting for the impeached. The managers strongly opposed Harper's appearing, and the Senate deliberated nearly all day on the admission of Harper. John Quincy Adams, a member of the Senate,† wrote that "the most determined and persevering opposition is made against having evidence and counsel to prove the man insane, only for fear that if insanity should be proved he cannot be convicted of high crimes and misdemeanors. Motion was made to assign him counsel to plead not guilty, and gave insanity as evidence in mitigation, as though an insane man could plead guilty or not guilty."‡ When the managers had retired from the Senate Chamber, the Senate heard Harper in support of the petition. He read affidavits in proof of Pickering's insanity, and he "humbly presumed, after testimony so direct and so conclusive, scarcely a doubt could possibly remain as to the insanity of this most unfortunate man; it cannot be necessary to prove that our laws except the insane from prosecution." Judge Pickering, Harper said, was insane at the time the offenses charged were committed, and he was ready to prove this if he should be allowed the privilege. He could show that before his loss of reason Judge Pickering had been a man of unquestioned purity, excellence and ability. "When this court shall take into consideration the situation of the respondent, oppressed with infirmities and incapable of making arrangement for his defense, the inclemency of the season, his great distance from the place of trial and the shortness of the notice; when your honors reflect on the high and atrocious crime with which he is charged, in the decision of which is involved not his life—his remains of life would be but a slender sacrifice—but that which is dearer than life itself, his good name; when you advert to the consequences

court's decision and said, "My decree is like those of the Medes and Persians, irrevocable." The counsel objected to this, and begged to be indulged with a few remarks. "Certainly," said the judge; "go on to all eternity."

*Annals of Congress, 1803-4, p. 327, Memoirs of John Quincy Adams, 1: 208.

†Memoirs, 1: 298.   ‡Memoirs, 1: 299.

of a conviction, the indelible stigma which will befall a
numerous family, whose only patrimony is the unsullied
reputation of their parent, when your honors shall think
of these things, the wisdom and justice of this court will
permit a respondent who is incapable of defending himself
to be defended by his friends." The dilemma of the managers was between the determination to remove the man on
impeachment, though he was insane, and the fear that the
evidence of his insanity and the argument of counsel might
affect the popularity of the measure. At least, so it seemed
to Senator Adams. He further adds that the managers
lamented that they had to present such a character as Pickering to the judgment of the Senate, but that the proof was
so strong and full against him that they should make no ob-
servation upon it.* The close of the trial is graphically described by John Quincy Adams.† "The time fixed for pro-
nouncing judgment was already past. The managers and
the whole House of Representatives were at the door of the
Senate waiting. Amid confusion and with precipitation a
form was adopted.‡ The doors were thrown open and the
whole House of Representatives came in with their Speaker
at their head. The question of guilty was taken on each
article separately." The result was each time the same, 19
yeas and 7 nays. The removal from office quickly followed
and the court adjourned. The second impeachment trial
was ended.

The first impeachment had concerned the legislative de-
partment of the Government. The second had to do with
the judicial branch. This was the first impeachment trial to
be carried through. Blount's case was managed by the Federalists. Pickering's trial was an attack of the victorious
Republicans upon the defeated Federalists. The same was
true in the Chase impeachment. The Federalists were
greatly alarmed at the result of Pickering's impeachment.
John Quincy Adams employed one day in writing to Colonel
Pickering of a plan of declaration to be subscribed by those
Senators who disapproved of the proceedings in the Pickering case.§ January 29, 1804, Pickering had written to
Cabot‖ that "Mr. Jefferson's plan of destruction has been

---

*Testimony for Judge Pickering might have been had in abundance
had Harper been heard by the managers.
†Memoirs, 1: 308.
‡Memoirs, 1: 297.
§Memoirs, 1: 303.
‖Lodge's Cabot, p. 337.

gradually advancing. I do not believe in the practicability of a long protracted union. A Northern Confederacy would unite congenial characters and present a better prospect of public happiness. I greatly doubt whether prudence should suffer the connection to continue much longer. The violation of the Constitution in the arbitrary removal of the judges may hasten such a crisis." The part taken by Harper in the Pickering impeachment was more a friendly effort in behalf of the helpless than the work of the advocate. His plea was not admitted by the managers, yet posterity is far from deciding against it.

The dramatic feature of the closing session of the Eighth Congress was the impeachment of Justice Chase. Upon its issue seemed to hang the last hope of the national judiciary, if not of the nation.* Chase was personally an upright, learned and able man, who had grown gray in his country's service. He had signed the Declaration of July 4, 1776.† He had been an ardent Democrat until Washington, against advice,‡ appointed him a Justice of the Supreme Court.§ He then became an ardent Federalist. His ill temper was the occasion of his trouble. His motives seemed to have been pure, but his actions were prejudiced by political opinion. In the charge to the grand jury in Baltimore‖ he used very extravagant and abusive language, and much of it was pointedly directed against the Republicans, then in power. In the court hearing the harangue was John Montgomery,¶ who wrote a letter to the *Baltimore American*, June 13, 1803, upon the liability to impeachment of Chase for alleged misbehavior in office. A cry for impeachment here begun found ready ears in Congress. John Randolph, of Roanoke, the Republican leader of the House, moved to impeach Chase (January 4, 1804). He reported (March 26, 1804), the eight articles of impeachment charging the Justice with acting on the bench in an arbitrary and unjust manner, so that a prisoner was condemned to death without having been defended by counsel, and with using rude expressions towards counsel,** and with delivering opinions highly inde-

---

*Schouler, History of the United States, 2, 76.
†Biography of the Signers, 9: 190.
‡Wharton, State Trials, p. 43.
§Spark's Washington, II, 107, 240.
‖May 2, 1803, Annals of Congress 1804-5, p. 675.
¶McMaster, History of the United States, 3, 170, Annals 1804-5, 231.
**These charges referred to the trial of Fries and Collendar in May, 1800, under the Alien and Sedition Laws.

ᵉent, tending to prostitute the judicial character with
which he was invested to the low purpose of an electioneer-
ing partisan. This was the real offense. The impeachment
court was held Jan. 2, 1805. Chase appeared and made a
speech and showed his characteristic ill temper by observ-
ing that they, the Congress of the United States, "were pul-
ing in their nurse's arms," whilst he was contributing his
utmost aid to lay the groundwork of American liberty.*
Aaron Burr was Vice-President and he "presided with the
impartiality of an angel and the rigor of a devil."† The
counsel for Chase were Harper, Joseph Hopkins, Philip B.
Key, Charles Lee, and Luther Martin. The trial began Feb.
4, 1805, and Harper and Hopkins presented the defense of
Chase. Chase's answer to the articles had been prepared
by Harper,‡ and maintained that there was no high crime
or misdemeanor particularly alleged in the articles to which
Chase was bound by law to answer,§ and that in the trial
of Fries if Chase erred he followed precedent and should
not therefore be held guilty.‖ Harper contended that only
civil officers are subject to impeachment and then only for
acts done in violation of some law. No civil officer can be
indicted except for an indictable offense. These were the
same views that he had set forth in the Blount case. To
the real onus of the impeachment, the political harangue
of the judge, Harper and Hopkinson replied that there was
no law which forbade such speeches, and without the
breach of some law there could be no impeachment.¶ It was
the very essence of despotism, they said, to punish for acts
which were forbidden by no law. Moreover, it had been
the practice ever since the Revolution** for the judges to
express from the bench by way of charge to the grand jury
political opinions. The Legislature had at times recommended the practice. It was adopted by the judges of the
Supreme Court, and by not forbidding it Congress had
given it an implied sanction.†† To punish the practice now
by impeachment was to make it a crime by ex post facto

---

*The preparations for the trial are graphically given by Charles
Evans, Report of the Trial of the Honorable Samuel Chase, &c., Bal-
timore, 1805, p. 3, Annals of Congress 1804-5, p. 100.
  †Parton, Life of Andrew Jackson, 1: 309.
  ‡Robert Walsh, Jr., Enc. Americana.
  §Annals 1804-5, p. 102.
  ‖Annals 1804-5, p. 109.
  ¶Annals 1804-5, pp. 146 and 305.
  **Annals 1804-5, pp. 146 and 305.
  ††Annals 1804-5, p. 147.

proceedings. John Randolph of Roanoke made an eloquent reply on the part of the Managers.* His line of argument was followed more or less closely by the other Managers. Luther Martin's argument for Chase was the climax of his career.† Harper went beyond his associates in narrowing the field of impeachment into a criminal prosecution, founded on the violation of some law. Everything with which they were surrounded in that chamber, he said, showed that it was a court of law and the whole transaction was a trial of a criminal case on legal principle. The Managers themselves resort to legal authorities to prove the acts charged to be impeachable offenses. The authorities sanctioned by the practice of one hundred and fifty years proves the principle for which Harper contended, both English and American legal authorities and the Constitution of the United States shows that impeachment is not an inquiry into the qualification of officers, but is a criminal prosecution of the violation of some law. No offense is impeachable unless it be proved to be the proper subject of indictment. "The Constitution is a limited branch of power not expressly or by necessary implication granted away. When, therefore, the Constitution declares for what act an officer shall be impeached, it gives power to impeach him for those acts, and all power to impeach him for any other act is withheld." "This provision of the Constitution, therefore, must be considered as a declaration that no impeachment shall lie, except for a criminal violation of some law." In the State Constitutions, also, impeachment has been considered a criminal prosecution for defined offenses. This is a sheet anchor or personal rights and political privileges. Without it everything is treason if tried before the party in power when unfavorable to the impeached. Nothing is treason when tried by friends. When the law defining offenses is fixed and certain every man is safe, but when passion and political views enter a trial justice is gone.

The effort of Harper and his colleagues were crowned with success. The principle that impeachment applied only to indictable offenses was sustained. The court declared that "Samuel Chase stands acquitted of all the articles exhibited against him."‡ It has been maintained that the impeachment of Justice Chase is a landmark in American history,

---

*Annals 1804-5, pp. 151 and 153.
†H. Adams, Hist. of U. S., 2, 232, Annals 1804-5, p. 429.
‡Annals 1804-5, p. 669.

because it overthrew the Jeffersonian Republicans in their last aggressive battle for the popular control of the judiciary.* The failure of the impeachment also overthrew the authority of John Randolph, of Roanoke. He hurried from the impeachment court to the House with an amendment to the Constitution providing that "the Judges of the Supreme Court and all other courts of the United States shall be removed by the President on the joint address by both Houses of Congress." Nicholson moved another' amendment that "The Legislature of any State might whenever it thought proper recall a Senator and vacate his seat.† In the opinion of Jefferson‡ it proved impeachment to be a mere scarecrow and "made a judiciary feel secure in undermining our confederated fabric by construing our Constitution from a co-ordination of a general and especial government to a general and supreme one alone." Marshall was henceforth safe in fixing his principles of Constitutional law. No point of law was decided by the trial. The theory of Randolph was still intact, while Harper and his colleagues were defeated neither by argument nor by the court's decision. Chase was declared innocent of any impeachable offence, and impeachment was seen to be an unwieldy instrument. It lay unused for a quarter of a century after this. The points insisted upon in these trials by Harper were: 1, that the impeached must be present; 2, that his presence may be compelled; 3, that a Senator is a civil officer and is liable to impeachment; 4, the impeached cannot escape trial by resignation or expulsion; 5, that the friends of the impeached may take up his defense if he is incapacitated; 6, that impeachment cannot be against those who are legally incapable of pleading guilty or not guilty; 7, that the English law and customs are to be observed as precedents in interpreting the Constitutional provisions; 8, only indictable offenses, violations of some law, are impeachable; 9, impeachment is not an inquiry into qualification for office, but is a criminal prosecution.

Harper left Congress with the downfall of the Federalists in March, 1801.

In May he was married to Miss Catherine Carroll, daughter of Charles Carroll, of Carrollton. Large debts growing out of land speculations had greatly interefered with his winning the hand of Miss Carroll. Her father was stren-

*H. Adams, Life of John Randolph. of Roanoke, p. 131.
†H. Adams, Hist. of the U. S., 2, 240; Hildreth, U. S., 5, 544.
‡Works 7, 192.

uously opposed to the match. But Harper now enjoyed the
good offices of Mr. Richard Caton, Mr. Carroll's son-in-law,
who knew how to sympathize with him. The correspondence between Mr. Carroll and Mr. Harper was straightforward and reflects credit upon Mr. Harper. It was under
these circumstances that Harper prepared the sketch of his
life, which has been used in this article.

He settled in Baltimore and devoted himself to his practice. His residence was on Gay street, near Water street.
Harper now enjoyed an income of from seven to ten thousand dollars a year, and his wife brought him a large dowery
in lands.

Soon after settling in Baltimore, Harper came out in a
pamphlet signed "Bystander," in which he advocated the
election of Presidential electors by the Legislature instead
of by popular vote. Roger Brooke Taney speaks of the
pamphlet as having the force and eloquence for which Harper was known. "It convinced me," he said, "and I at once
took grounds in favor of the measure. Some of the Federalists objected to it, and it was attacked by the friends of Mr.
Jefferson."*

Justice Story frequently saw Harper in Washington at
the Supreme Court, and describes him as "diffuse, but me-
thodical and clear. He argues with considerable warmth,
and seems to depend upon the deliberate suggestions of his
mind. I am inclined to think he studies his cases with great
diligence, and is to be considered as in some degree arti-
ficial."†

Baltimore, at the time of Harper's locating there, was a
town of 31,000 people,‡ but it was without an adequate water
supply. Wells and springs were depended upon.§ In April,
1804, Harper was appointed on a committee, embracing
many familiar names in the city's history, to report a plan
and constitution of a water company.‖ Harper and others
were appointed to open subscription books for the stock.
But only when they had used their personal influence was
the stock taken and the company organized, May 24, 1804.
The directors of the company were John McKim, Sr., James
A. Buchanan, Jonathan Ellicott, Solomon Etting, John Don-

---

*Tyler, Memoir of Taney, p. 91.
†Story, "Life of W. W. Story," 1: 162, 214, 252, 279.
‡Griffith, "Annals of Baltimore."
§Scharf, "Baltimore City and County," p. 213.
‖Griffith, "Annals of Baltimore, p. 3, 171. Scharf, "Baltimore City
and County." p. 213.

nell, William Cooke, James Mosher and Robert Goodloe
Harper.* The Baltimore Water Company remained in existence until 1853.†

In 1815 Harper co-operated with prominent business men
in forming The Baltimore Exchange Company. January 25,
1816, the company was incorporated and authorized to erect
the Baltimore Exchange. Harper was one of the first Board
of Directors.‡ The exchange was said at the time to have
had no rival in America. Benj. H. Latrobe, the architect of
the cathedral, furnished the design.§

Harper was not only public-spirited, and interested in the
improvement of his adopted city, he also took great interest
in its social affairs. In 1810 we find him one of the managers of the Baltimore Dancing Assembly. The assembly was
an old organization. The lower floor of the assembly rooms
at Holliday and Fayette streets was occupied by the Baltimore Library Company. In this company were William
Wirt, Archbishop Carroll, J. P. Kennedy, Robert Goodloe
Harper, William Gwynn and others. The home of William
Gwynn was also the home of the earliest Baltimore club,
the Delphian Club, which met at "Gwynn's Folly" or "Tuscu-
lum," in the rear of Barnum's Hotel. Some of the papers
of the Delphian Club may still be seen in their "Red Book,"
which was published fortnightly during 1818-1819. Harper
was a member of the Delphian Club, and there met with
John Neal, later a writer for Blackwood's Magazine, and
who spoke in praise of Harper's writings; Jared Sparks, the
historian and biographer, who ably supported Harper's colonization plans,‖ and Francis Scott Key. The list of distinguished associates Harper found at the Delphian Club is
long, and includes the authors of such familiar verses as
"Home, Sweet Home," "Old Oaken Bucket," "Airs of Pales-
tine," and "Rock Me to Sleep, Mother."¶

In General Harper's law office in 1808 was Robert Walsh,
Jr. (1784-1859), who afterwards wrote for Francis Lieber's
Americana Encyclopedia a biographical sketch of Harper,
among other Americans. Walsh, in 1811, started the first
quarterly ever published in the United States, "The American Review of History and Politics." The Review only

*Griffith, "Annals of Baltimore," 171.
†Scharf, "Baltimore City and County," 215.
‡Griffith, "Annals of Baltimore," 214.
§Scharf, "Baltimore City and County," 437.
‖North American Review, Jan. 1824.
¶Scharf, "Baltimore City and County."

lived two years. In November, 1810, Walsh wrote to Harper that the Review was recommended by the most distinguished Federalists, and he hoped it would meet with Harper's approval. "I shall rely on your assistance in promoting the work not only in Baltimore, but in the South, where you have so many friends."*

At a dinner in Georgetown, June 5, 1813, in honor of recent Russian victories, Harper gave as a toast "Alexander the Deliverer." Walsh replied to this speech when published, claiming that the military character of Napoleon had been underrated, and that Harper had failed to point out the dangers of Russian ascendancy. This provoked a long correspondence, which was published. Walsh says that General Harper was a diligent student of literature, history, geography, travels, statistics, moral philosophy, political science, and especially of political economy. No one was better acquainted with foreign affairs than General Harper.

In 1814, Harper published two columns of "Select Works." These consist of speeches on political and forensic subjects, and political tracts, which had previously appeared as pamphlets or addresses.†

His "Observations on the Dispute with France," Walsh says, "acquired great celebrity at home and passed through several editions in England, and was esteemed over Europe one of the ablest productions of the crisis."

In 1819-1820 General Harper made an extensive tour in England, France and Italy.‡ In 1820 Princeton College conferred upon him the degree of Doctor of Laws.§ Robert

*MS. letter in Johns Hopkins University, in "Walsh's Appeal from the Judgment of Great Britain," 1819, the first pro-slavery work ever published.

†Among the titles are "Address to His Constituents," a defense of the Jay Treaty, Philadelphia, 1795; "Observations on the Dispute between the United States and France," London, 1797; "Correspondence with George Nicholas on His Political Conduct in the Sixth Congress," Lexington, Ky., 1799; "Correspondence with Robert Walsh, Jr.," Philadelphia, 1813; "Address in Favor of the Potomac Canal," 1824; "Oration on the Birth of Washington," Alexandria, 1810; "Speech at the Celebration of the Recent Triumph of Mankind in Germany," Alexandria, 1814; "Letter to the Colonization Society," Baltimore, 1818; and "Arguments on the Blount and Chase Impeachments."

‡While in Rome a bust of the General was executed by Trentanove. Copies of this bust, which is in the possession of Dr. Clapham Pennington, are at the Peabody Library, Maryland Historical Society's Rooms, and in the Johns Hopkins University.

§Letter from Dr. J. O. Murray, Princeton University, February 10, 1898.

Walsh describes him at this time as being above the middle
stature, well shaped, muscular, erect and active in habits. He
was warm-hearted, tender and generous. He gave aid,
praise and sympathy, showed elegant hospitality and enjoyed young and gay society. He was a brilliant conversa-
tionalist; an animated and sufficiently fluent and very per-
spicuous orator. He had a facility in applying general principles and in seizing the moment of excited curiosity for ex-
hibiting motives or consequences.

When the British attacked Baltimore in 1814, Harper,
who had held a commission in a voluntary artillery company,* greatly exerted himself at the battle of North Point.
He was in the hottest of the fight.† In October, 1814, he
was commissioned Major-General of the forces of Maryland.
When the corner-stone of the Battle Monument was laid,
September 13, 1815, General Harper was in command,‡ and
likewise on the occasion of the laying of the corner-stone of
the Washington Monument, July 4, 1816.

When Lafayette visited Baltimore in 1824, General Harper
took a prominent part in the very elaborate ceremonies.§

On January 27, 1816, General Harper was elected United
States Senator by the Senate and House of Delegates of
Maryland.‖ The Senator took his seat February 5, 1816.¶
No measure of great importance arose during the session,
but wherever issues arose Harper was heard. A few days
after his entrance he gave notice of his intention to bring
in a bill for the establishment of a law library at the Capital,** for the use of the Supreme Court of the United States;
and, also, a bill for limiting the right of appeal and writ of
error from the Circuit Court of the United States.†† An
amendment to the Constitution had been proposed regarding the mode of choosing Representatives and Electors. Har-

*Griffith, "Annals of Baltimore," 212.

†Parkins, "History of the War of 1812, 341. Niles' Register.

‡Scharf, "Baltimore City and County," p. 268.

§Mr. Levasseur, Lafayette in Amerique, 2: 1, described the occasion:

"Le Général Harper ouvrit la séance par un discours fort instruc-
tif sur les progrès et l'état actuel de l'agriculture dans le Maryland * * * Le même jour (Dimanche) le corps d'officiers des
milices fut presenté par le général Harper, qui prononça un discours
dont le passage suivant me parut tout à fait remarquâble," etc.

‖Votes and proceedings of the Senate, page 3, of the House, page
8, December session, 1816.

¶Benton, "Abridgment," 5: 460.

**Annals of Congress, 1816-17, p. 136.

††Annals of Congress, 1816, p. 136.

per was a supporter of the proposed change, on the ground
that the amendment would make the election of the President less a matter of juggle and intrigue than it then was.
Party bargains would not be so easy between state and state
for the great offices. Districting the states for the election
of Electors would tend to render the choice more free and
independent.* He opposed the election of the President
solely by the popular vote, because that threw out of view
the Federal principle by which the sovereignty of the states
were represented. It would destroy the influence of the
smaller states and multiply the principle of compromise on
which our Constitution rests.† When a bill was presented
for the incorporation of the Washington Female Orphan
Asylum Harper opposed it, because he thought it contrary
to the whole course of our laws, and a strange anomaly to
see a body politic made up wholly of married women.‡ The
proposed change of pay to Senators and Representatives
from six dollars a day to fifteen hundred dollars a year and
to deduct from this an amount in proportion for absence or
irregularity was opposed by some as being extravagant. It
would double former allowances and would be larger pay
than many of the states give to their principal officers. The
change proposed found a champion in Harper, and it was
carried.§ Although the session of the Senate afforded General Harper no adequate field for his abilities, yet a speech
he made April 4 is noteworthy when read in the light of recent events. The occasion was a proposed amendment to a
navigation bill introduced by Mr. Bibb, of the Committee on
Foreign Affairs.‖ The bill proposed to confine American
navigation to American seamen. Harper's amendment to
this had for its object the gradual exclusion from the navy
and from the merchant service all those who were not native or at that time already naturalized citizens of the United
States,¶ and also the compelling of merchant vessels to keep
on board a number of American apprentices. The exclusion
of foreign sailors, he said, would save us from more trouble
about impressment, and the American apprentices would
furnish skillful seamen in time of war, especially war with

---

*Annals, 1816-17; p. 221.
†Annals, 1816-17; p. 225.
‡Annals, p. 189.
§Annals, 1816, 1817; p. 203.
‖Annals, p. 372.
¶Annals, 1815-16; p. 229. He later withdrew his amendment, An-
nals, p. 297.

England, then apparently impending.* The United States asserted it as a right to incorporate foreigners into our nation by naturalizing them. This drew them from their native allegiance. The United States had made an advance beyond other nations in holding that these naturalized citizens of hers must be protected to the same extent as native citizens. England had from time immemorial held that allegiance is perpetual; that it cannot be alienated save by consent of sovereign and subject both. All other governments but the United States held the same doctrine. How far would it be wise to contest these principles when the universal opinion of mankind, save in the United States, was against it? Zeal and sacrifice of person and property could only be expected of men in a case of which they approve.† We could not expect always to remain in peace. Conflicts from time to time with England seemed inevitable. The important matter was to be ready. Future conflicts would be on the sea, and on the sea we were destined at the last to be the supreme power.‡ "There is the true scene of our glory." The best support of the power was not ships, nor money, but a brave, hardy and numerous class of native and patriotic seamen. It was the man behind the gun. These money cannot buy. Hirelings can never do what brave patriots will do.

Before the end of the year (December 1, 1816), General Harper, finding that a conscientious discharge of public duties would rob him wholly of time for his private concerns, resigned his seat in the Senate.§ He retired to private life and the management of his business.

At the election in 1816, Harper had received the votes of Delaware for Vice-President of the United States, and again in 1820.

On the western coast of Africa is the home of a unique nation. The history of this nation tells of helpless human creatures, stolen from savagery and carried with untold sufferings over the sea to be sold as chattels. Slowly exchanging there in patient servitude savagery for civilization, they unconsciously drew near to a higher destiny. Again they crossed the sea, not as naked savages worth so

---

*Annals, p. 284.
†Annals, p. 284.
‡Annals, p. 292.
§December session, 1816, Maryland House of Delegates; Votes and Proceedings, Senate, p. 3; House, p. 8.

much cash, but as carriers of the benefits of civilization to their original home.

To-day these ex-slaves are a free, independent nation, occupying a territory three times as large as the State of Virginia. Their population of nearly two millions live under a government modeled after that of the greatest of republics. With creating this peculiar nation General Harper had much to do. Whether the scheme was Utopian or not is of no consequence. The colony of Liberia must ever be of interest as the first and only colony planted by the United States. Liberia is of far greater interest as an attempt to cure the sore on the body politic; an attempt which might have prevented the paroxysm of 1861-5 and settled a question which looms upon the horizon to-day.

It may be plainly shown from the writings of Washington, Jefferson, Madison, Henry, Mason and many others that there long existed a desire in the South for the abolition of negro slavery. The desire did not ripen into a definite plan.

On January 2, 1800, a petition was presented to Congress by the free blacks of Philadelphia, in which they protested against the slave trade, and asked for legislation in behalf of fugitive slaves and for steps looking to the emancipation of slaves.

This petition was successfully opposed by John Randolph, of Roanoke, and Robert Goodloe Harper, on the ground that it was prompted by religious fanaticism, and that Congress had no power to act in the premises.*

Harper's opposition was not, however, due to any pro-slavery views, for on May 3 he advocated the abolition of the slave trade between the United States and any foreign country.†

The Virginia Legislature, December 31, 1800, in consequence of a slave conspiracy about Richmond, secretly requested Governor Monroe to correspond with the President of the United States on the subject of buying lands without the limits of the United States, whither "persons obnoxious to the laws and dangerous to the peace of society may be removed."‡

Mr. Jefferson favored the plan, and corresponded with the British Government concerning Sierra Leone and with Spain regarding lands in South America. These attempts failed,

---

*"Benton's Abridgment," 2: 430.
†"Benton's Abridgment," 2: 439.
‡"Benton's Abridgment," 2: 477.

and January 22, 1805, an effort was made to secure lands in Louisiana.*

Jefferson's views are given in a letter to John Lynd, January 21, 1811, in which he declares he has "ever thought that Colonization in Africa the most desirable measure for drawing off this part of our population." "Nothing is more to be wished," he says in another letter, "than that the United States would themselves undertake to make such an establishment on the coast of Africa."

One of the greatest obstacles in the way of manumission of the slaves was the wretched condition of the free blacks. Jared Sparks said that "the free people of color are a greater nuisance to society, more comfortless, tempted to more vices, and actually less qualified to enjoy existence than the savages themselves."†

John Randolph, of Roanoke, was of the opinion that "thousands of citizens would by manumitting their slaves relieve themselves from the cares attendant upon their possession, if there were only some means of disposing of the free blacks.‡

Here there arose the need of a movement towards colonization and of colonization on a large scale. This movement was undertaken by the American Society for the Colonization of the Free People of Color.

Rev. Robert Finley was the founder of the American Colonization Society. He went to Washington, and succeeded in gathering a meeting of citizens December 21, 1816. Henry Clay presided at this meeting.§ The society was regularly organized and officered January 1, 1817.‖

---

*See "Mercer's Report," March 3, 1827, Nineteenth Congress, second session; House Reports, No. 101, and Birney's Colonization Pamphlets, 1824-1833, Vol. 19, and Kennedy's Report, 1843.

†H. B. Adams' "Life and Writings of Jared Sparks," 1: 248.

‡Mercer's Report, Nineteenth Congress, second session, House Reports No. 101, p. 30. Virginia kept at the question until her Legislature memorialized Congress December 23, 1816. Maryland, Tennessee and Georgia followed. H. B. Adams, Life and Writings of Jared Sparks, 1: 252.

§Dr. Finley had left Princeton about the time Harper was at college. He was afterwards President of the University of Georgia. He published "Thoughts on the Colonization of the Free Blacks." 1816. "Memoirs of Rev. Robt. Finley, D. D.," etc. By Rev. Isaac V. Brown, A. M. New Brunswick, 1819.

‖The first officers of the society were Bushrod Washington, William H. Crawford, Henry Clay, John Eager Howard and Andrew Jackson. Other members were Daniel Webster, John Randolph of Roanoke, Francis Scott Key and C. F. Mercer. The Presidents of

Samuel J. Mills, in 1808, organized at Williams College, for missionary work, a society, which was soon transferred to Andover and became eventually the American Bible Society and the American Board of Foreign Missions. The idea of Mills was to colonize negroes between the Ohio and the lakes, or in Africa. When Mills went to study theology at Princeton he interested the Presbyterian ministers in his scheme and among them Dr. Finley.*

General Harper was among the original members.†

In 1803, Mr. Latrobe executed a painting of the society's colony, "Maryland in Liberia," and hung it in the Senate Chamber at Annapolis.‡

The society declared its objects to be to promote and execute a plan for colonizing, with their consent, the free people of color in Africa or such other place as Congress should designate.§ This was the first and only society ever organized for the explicit purpose of giving the negro perfect freedom, of promoting his education for rhis own good, of making him independent, and of elevating his race to the standard of a Christian nation.||

But the society met with great opposition¶ both from slavery advocates, who feared an interference with their rights, and from anti-slavery men, who feared that the society was working in the interest of the slave trade to raise the price of slaves by reducing their number. Nearly all the noted abolitionists after 1831 had been before that colonizationists.

Benjamin Lundy's travels through North America had been for the purpose of finding a location for a free black colony in Texas or in Mexico. James G. Birney was the society's agent for Alabama and Tennessee.**

It was William Lloyd Garrison, a printer from Massachusetts, who had worked for Lundy as publisher of "Genius of Universal Emancipation" in Baltimore, who made war on the colonization scheme, 1829-30,

the society have been Bushrod Washington, 1817-1830; Charles Carroll of Carrollton, 1830-1833; James Madison, 1833-1836; Henry Clay, 1836-1853; J. H. B. Latrobe, 1853-1891; Bishop H. C. Potter, 1891-1898. (A. C. S. Reports and "Liberia.")

*Johns Hopkins University Studies 9: 497.

†J. H. B. Latrobe's address in the "Semi-Centennial Report," A. C. S., 1867.

‡Baltimore American. March 10, 1885.

§A. C. S. Reports, 1818, 1; 1.

||A. N. Bell, The Debt of Africa, the Hope of Liberia, 1881.

¶This line of division was intensified until it became the great chasm opening towards the Civil War.

**Alexander Johnston in Lalor 1: 3.

and in his fiery zeal for immediate and unconditional emancipation fanned fanaticism to a white heat.

Under these circumstances General Harper came to the
rescue of the society, and defended it against both classes
of opposers. August 20, 1817, he wrote a long letter, in
which he set forth the advantages of colonization to the
blacks themselves. He showed that the first gain of all
would be to our own people by ridding us of the idle and
vicious class of free blacks. They are condemned to a hopeless degradation by their color, which is an indelible mark
of their origin. This mark establishes forever an impassable
barrier between them and the whites. This barrier rests
upon our habits, our feelings, on our prejudices, but whether
prejudice or feelings it makes us recoil from the idea of an
intimate union with the free blacks. A state of equality
between the races, which alone could make us one people,
is simply impossible. Be their industry ever so good, their
conduct ever so correct, their property ever so great, we may
admire their character; we never could consent and they
never could hope to see the two races placed on a footing
of perfect equality with each other. They never could visit
our homes or participate in public honors and employment.
This is strictly true of every part of our country, even of
those parts where slavery has long ceased to exist and is
held in abhorrence.

"There is no State in the Union," General Harper said,
"where a negro or mulatto can ever hope to be a member of
Congress, a judge, or a militia officer, or even a justice of the
peace; to sit down at the table with respectable whites or
mix freely in their society.

"Paul Cuffee,* respectable, intelligent and wealthy, has no
chance of ever being invited to dine with a gentleman in
Boston or of marrying his daughter, whatever may be her
education or fortune, to one of their sons."

These passages are very striking in the light of subse-
quent developments, claims and accomplished facts. General Harper goes on in his argument to show how different
slavery in the United States was from servitude in any other
country, and why the liberated slave found his lot so much

---

*Paul Cuffee, of Boston, son of an Indian woman, and a native
African father, was born off the coast of Massachusetts. He became
a sailor, then a trader, and acquired wealth. He was an influential
Quaker. He manned his vessels wholly with negroes. In 1811 he
went in his own ship to Sierra Leone to study its condition, and in
1815 he took out 38 negro emigrants at his own expense. A second
expedition was interrupted by his death.

harder than that of freedmen in other countries and other ages.

Slavery then existed in more than three-fourths of the globe, but the great body of slaves everywhere, except in America, were of the same race, origin and color, and of the same general character as the free men. So it was among the ancients. Under such conditions manumission not only removed the slave from the condition of slavery, but also exempted him from its consequences and opened the way for a full participation in all the privileges of freedom. He was raised to an equality with the free class, and might wash out the stains of his former degradation and obliterate its memory. In the United States, General Harper said, this is impossible, for you may manumit the slave, but you cannot make him a white man. He still remains a negro, and the mark of his former condition still adheres to him and forms a barrier which can never be removed. The debasement which was formerly compulsory becomes habitual and voluntary. Far better was the condition of a well-cared-for slave than that of the wretched freedman. As long as the freedman existed in the midst of slavery he was not only hopeless, but he was a corrupting influence upon slaves and a constant menace to order. General Harper urged that to remove this class from their position of danger to society and of hopelessness and put them in an environment suited to their needs was the most reasonble solution of the problem. And colonization was aiming at just this result. Moreover, colonization would tend, he claimed, to rid the people of the United States entirely of slaves and slavery. From this point of view colonization most strongly appealed to him and to the world for support. "No person," he says, "who has seen the slave-holding States and those where slavery does not exist can have failed to have been struck with the difference in favor of the latter. In population, in general diffusion of wealth and comfort, in education, manners and mode of life of the middle class, in roads, bridges and rivers, in schools and churches, and in general advancement, there was no comparison. The change is apparent the instant you cross the line which separates the country where there are slaves and where there are none."

General Harper was of the opinion that to substitute a free white class of laborers for slaves was as practicable as it would be beneficial, and that colonization was the first step in this direction. All emancipation which permits the emancipated person to remain in this country was an evil;

for it to extend to the whole black race would be intolerable. But he gave his hearty support to a society which would open the way for colonization and thereby relieve the country of the impending evil. If the freed blacks could be colonized in Africa they would become free in fact and would have no hindrance from a white population reminding them of their former degradation.*

This fact would induce more frequent manumission, and this in turn would have a good effect upon the slaves. Moreover, the gain to commerce would be great and, above all, would be the beneficent effect upon Africa from this return of her own race, carrying knowledge and civilization with them.

Some persons advocated the sending of colonists to Sierra Leone, but General Harper opposed this on the ground of the greater advance in geographical knowledge of Africa. We ought to profit, he said, by the misfortune of Sierra Leone, and make first choice of locations, and lay a sure foundation good for the distant future. Indeed, the colony should be as distant as possible from Sierra Leone, in order to avoid any complication with its people.†

He wished to see "our colony republican and fashioned with a view to self-government and independence, at the earliest possible period, for thus only can it be most useful to the colonists, to Africa and to us." His foresight in the choice of a proper site for the colony assured its future. It must be in communication with the Niger river, destined, he said, to be the connecting channel between interior Africa and the world.‡

Above all, Harper insisted upon the choice of a place that would be strategic for the future. He believed in the future of Africa, and at the end of his letter allowed his feelings to burst out in anticipation of the "hope of success which seems sufficient to stimulate us to the utmost exertion. Who can count the millions that in a future time shall know and bless

---

*One of the causes of the prejudices at present existing in Liberia between the native Africans and the Afro-Americans is the oft-heard taunt from the natives of "Slave" applied to the natives of Liberia. Fred. Douglass in Johnson's Encyclopedia.

†Failure to follow this suggestion of General Harper led to independence of Liberia, July 6, 1847.

‡He relied for information of the geography of Africa upon Park, Maxwell, Riley and other travelers. Geography had been a favorite study with him. His wide knowledge of it and his experience as a surveyor were now of great service to him. His choice of Mesurado, instead of Sherbrough, was amply justified in the sequel.

the names of those by whom this magnificent scheme has been conceived and shall be carried into execution? Throughout the widely extended regions of Middle and Southern Africa, then filled with populous and polished natives, their praises shall be sung when other States shall have run their round of grandeur and decay, and shall no longer be known, except by vague report of their former greatness."

General Harper's views created a profound impression and assured the success of the society. Jared Sparks wrote in the North American Review, January, 1824: "General Harper's views are philosophical, just in principle and fact."

His suggestions were acted on in the fall of 1817, and an exploring party was sent to Africa. The expedition so drained the society that it might have been ruined but for the help of President Monroe,* who, by a liberal construction of an act of Congress, co-operated with the society, and $33,000 was put at their disposal. Eighty-six negroes were sent out and arrived in Africa in March, 1829. Most of them did not survive the fever. Twenty-eight more were sent March, 1821. In April, 1822, the first permanent settlement was made. The struggle for life against the climate and the natives makes a thrilling story which cannot be related here.†

February, 1824, the "Cyrus" took out one hundred and three negroes from about Petersburg, Richmond and Norfolk, Va. The "Oswego," May, 1823, had carried two negroes, freed in order that they might go to Liberia, the "Cyrus" had eleven such; while in 1824 the "Nautilus" carried one hundred and forty-nine such.‡ The cost of transportation was as low as $26 a head.§ The funds of the society were gotten from the annual fee of one dollar, the life fee of $30 and from legacies and gifts. Koskiusko left $20,000 for young negro women. This was used to buy a farm for training children for the colony.‖ Rev. William Meade, later Bishop Meade, collected much money in Virginia and the South for the society. General Harper was a liberal contributor and also gave many books, maps and papers for the society.

When the question came up of asking aid of the United

*J. H. U. Studies, 9: 500.
†In 1821 Dr. Ely Ayres, agent for the society, was sent out in a United States vessel under Lieutenant Stockton. Ayres and Stockton bought of King Peter, King George, King Zoda, King Long Peter, King Governor and King Jimmy, for $300, a tract of land for the colony. A. C. S. Reports, 7, 79, 1824.
‡Table of Recaptured Africans, &c., Washington, 1845.
§Christian Examiner, 1824, pp. 83, 467.
‖Christian Examiner, 1824, p. 322.

States Government for the society, General Harper warmly supported the claim the society had upon the Government. No private means, he said, could carry out the scheme of the society. All they could do was to pave the way. It had been shown to be practicable to colonize the free blacks. But private efforts could at most reach only a few thousand of them. The task needed a far mightier hand, and it must have three indispensable features; it must be gradual, voluntary and with consent of the slave owners. Such a task required national means. The object was national in its consequences. The nation must remove the national evil. "We may appeal to the patriotism and good sense of Congress," he said, "in this great national undertaking."*

When the society met, February, 1824, General Harper proposed a name for the African colony—Liberia. "A name that is peculiar, short and familiar and that expresses the object and nature of the establishment in Liberia, which denotes a settlement of people made free. This name is easy, apt and concise." The name was adopted. Then General Harper proposed to call the capital "Monrovia," "as a mark of gratitude to that venerable man to whom it owes more than to any other single man, it being perfectly well known that but for the favorable use of the great powers confided to him all our efforts must have been unavailing."† The town, now Cape Palmas, the home of the Kroomen,‡ was named Harper by the society for the man who named the country and the capital.§

In twenty years the society sent out more than four thousand negroes. Of these sixteen hundred were from Virginia and seven hundred and seventy-five from North Carolina.

In 1896 emigration, which had been checked by the Civil War, began to revive, and three hundred and twenty-five went on their own charges.‖ Since 1822 the total number of emigrants sent to Liberia is 18,000. Liberia has never really been a part of Africa; it has been more a part of Virginia or North Carolina, stuck on to the African coast. American ideas and sentiments prevail to the total exclusion of social aspirations. Yet the Americo-Liberians, as they prefer to be called, have done a great work for Africa.

The emigrants and their descendants number only about

*Lincoln, December 1, 1862, favored colonization of free negroes outside the United States, Selox, 1; 5.
†J. H. U. Studies, p. 511; A. C. S. Reports, 7: 5.
‡Fred Douglass in Johnson's Encyclopedia.
§J. H. U. Studies, 9: 511.
‖Liberia, Bulletin of A. C. S.,. February, 1897, p. 4.

20,000, but their sphere of influence extends over thousands of natives. They have demonstrated the capacity of the negro for self-government, if given the proper environment.*

Liberia has four counties, Mesurado, Grand Basso, Senoie, and Maryland in Liberia; Louisiana, New Georgia, Virginia, Greenville and Lexington. There is no national debt, a surplus in the treasury, a property qualification for the suffrage, a regular school system and churches of various denominations.

The exhibit from Liberia at the World's Fair was very creditable. The direct trade of Liberia with the United States is not large, but the use of American goods bought in Europe is considerable.

To all the results of the scheme of colonization General Harper contributed more or less. In particular his part in the work may be briefly capitulated, thus:

1. He was one of the early members of the society.

2. His able defense of the society at a critical moment turned the trend of opinion to an interest in the plan.

3. He was for years a vice-president of the society.

4. He was Vice-President of the Maryland Auxiliary Society.

5. He gave the names Liberia and Monrovia to the land and its capital.

6. His own name has been given to the town of Harper.†

Of General Harper as a lawyer we have had little to say. The aim and the limits of this paper preclude an account of that side of his activity. His practice was large, important and lucrative. Mention of a few cases will illustrate his

---

*Fred Douglass in Johnson's Encyclopedia.

†The American Colonization Society still exists. It has accomplished these results:

1. It established a colony, which exists to-day as an independent nation.

2. It has given aid to emigrants.

3. It has diffused knowledge of Africa and of the free blacks of the United States.

4. It has aroused sympathy for the negro race in the United States and in Africa.

5. It checked the slave trade.

6. It has aided in the civilization and Christianization of Africa.

7. It made an honest effort to cure our country's evils.

8. It may yet furnish the solution for the greatest problem which confronts our people.

Captain Cameron, R. N., has said, "Africa is the hope of the future and will be the salvation of an over-crowded world." (A. C. S. Reports, 1897, page 80.)

line of work. In 1809-1810 he was engaged with John Quincy Adams on the case of Fletcher vs. Peck, before the Supreme Court of the United States. In the Pennsylvania Supreme Court he was associated with Tilgman, Rawle and Lewis, in the case of Commonwealth vs. Cobbett, in 1798. In the Maryland courts the records and reports show that he took part in 1803 in the case of Owings vs. Smith with Luther Martin, the "Bulldog," as his opponent, and the next year he was with Martin against Ingersoll and Lincoln and Dallas in the case of Pennington vs. Coxe. This list might be greatly extended. The part Harper played in impeachment trials has been referred to above.

In 1824 General Harper determined to retire from professional life, and devote himself to public concerns. The broad and liberal principles he espoused were set forth in an address at the time he announced himself for Congress. In the midst of these plans sudden death came.* General Harper died January 14, 1825.† His funeral ceremonies were most elaborate,‡ and testified to the universal esteem in which he was held in his own city.§

General Harper's death called forth many warm tributes of respect. The American Colonization Society spoke of him as "a friend whose splendid talents commanded the respect of the loftiest, whose warm, practical and efficient benevo-

---

*Niles' Register, January 22, 1825, p. 986.

†See account of his sudden death in J. P. Kennedy, "Life of William Wirt, 2, 169, where is quoted a letter of Wirt's, January 16, 1825.

‡Baltimore American, January 17, 1825.

§A full account of it may be seen in a rare old book by Jos. Pickering, "An Emigrant's Guide to Canada." My thanks are due to Mr. Bump of the Baltimore Sun for the use of this book.

General Harper was interred at his county estate "Oakland." His remains were later removed to Greenmount Cemetery in Baltimore. The monument there bears the epitaph:

ROBERT GOODLOE HARPER.

Born near Fredericksburg, Virginia. A member of the Legislature of South Carolina. Then a Representative of that State in Congress. Then chosen to the Senate of Maryland. And then a Senator from Maryland in the Senate of the United States. As a statesman he was distinguished by extended knowledge, accurate judgment, energy of character, and unbending integrity. As a lawyer he occupied an exalted station at the Bar of Maryland. As husband, father and friend he possessed and exercised all the warm and noble feelings of the human heart. He died at Baltimore, January 14, 1825, in the sixty-first year of his age. "Vir cui ad summam auctoritatem nihil defuit praeter sanam civium mentem." Tit. Liv.

lence, the affection of the purest minds."* The most elaborate and eloquent tribute was pronounced by William Wirt, who said: "He has been for thirty years on the great theater of the United States and in the eyes of the nation; * * * the nation has considered him as one of her brightest ornaments. We are proud to acknowledge him as standing in the van of our ranks, who would have thrown an illustrious light upon the profession in any country."† John Neal in Blackwood's Magazine said of Harper: "We hold him to be altogether one of the ablest men North America has produced."‡

*A. C. S., Reports, 8:4, 19. Missionary Herald, vol. 21, April, 1825.
†Niles' Register, January 22, 1825, p. 986.
‡Vol. 17, p. 56.